Mr. Putter & Tabby
Take the Train

CYNTHIA RYLANT

Mr. Putter & Tabby Take the Train

Illustrated by

ARTHUR HOWARD

🐦 sandpiper

HOUGHTON MIFFLIN HARCOURT
Boston   New York

For Paula
—A. H.

All rights reserved. Published in the United States by Sandpiper, an imprint of
Houghton Mifflin Harcourt Publishing Company.
Originally published in hardcover in the United States by
Harcourt Children's Books, an imprint of Houghton Mifflin Harcourt
Publishing Company, 2008

SANDPIPER and the SANDPIPER logo are trademarks of
Houghton Mifflin Harcourt Publishing Company.

For information about permission to reproduce selections from this book, write to trade.
permissions@hmhco.com or to Permissions, Houghton Mifflin Harcourt Publishing
Company, 3 Park Avenue, 19th Floor, New York, New York 10016.

www.hmhco.com

The illustrations in this book were done in pencil,
watercolor, and gouache on 250-gram cotton rag paper.
The display type was set in Minya Nouvelle, Agenda, and Artcraft.
The text type was set in Berkeley Old Style Book.

The Library of Congress has cataloged the hardcover edition as follows:
Rylant, Cynthia.
Mr. Putter & Tabby take the train/Cynthia Rylant;
illustrated by Arthur Howard.
p.   cm.
Summary: After a small setback, Mr. Putter and his favorite
companions enjoy the best train ride of their lives.
[1. Trains—Fiction.   2. Cats—Fiction.   3. Dogs—Fiction.
4. Old age—Fiction.]
I. Howard, Arthur, ill.   II. Title.
PZ7.R982Mg   1998
[E]—dc21   97-23471
ISBN 978-0-15-201786-6
ISBN 978-0-15-202389-8 (pb)

Manufactured in China

SCP 20 19 18 17 16 15 14 13 12 11 10
4500634692

1

An Idea

One day Mr. Putter and his
fine cat, Tabby, were cooking some
oatmeal when Mrs. Teaberry called.

Mrs. Teaberry was Mr. Putter's
friend and neighbor.
"I have an idea!" she told
Mr. Putter.

As she spoke, her good dog, Zeke,
wagged at Tabby through
the window.
(Tabby and Zeke were friends
and neighbors, too.)

Mr. Putter was not sure he
wanted to hear Mrs. Teaberry's idea.
Sometimes her ideas were odd
and involved running fast,
or wearing feathers,

or having purple toes.

But Mr. Putter always had good
manners, so he asked,
"What is your idea, Mrs. Teaberry?"
(Though he really didn't want to know.)
"I think we should
take a train!"
said Mrs. Teaberry.

A train, thought Mr. Putter.

Mr. Putter loved trains.

When he was a boy,
he rode them all the time.
He loved the big windows
and smooth seats
and traveling backwards.
But he hadn't been
on a train in years.

"I haven't been on a train in years,"
he told Mrs. Teaberry.
"Exactly!" said Mrs. Teaberry.
"Let's go tomorrow.
We'll go north for two hours
then turn around and come back."

Mr. Putter looked at Tabby, who
was still waiting for her oatmeal.
"Can we bring Tabby and Zeke?"
Mr. Putter asked Mrs. Teaberry.

"Of course!" she said.

"You're sure pets are allowed?" he asked.

"Certainly!"

"And they can sit with us
on the train?" Mr. Putter asked.

"Of course they can!" said
Mrs. Teaberry.

"You're sure," said Mr. Putter.

"I'm sure," said Mrs. Teaberry.

"Positive?" asked Mr. Putter.

"Positive," said Mrs. Teaberry.

"Pets," she declared, "can go on trains!"

2

Another Idea

"I'm sorry," said the ticket
woman the next day.
"Pets can't go on trains."

"WHAT?" said Mrs. Teaberry.

Zeke was standing beside her
wearing his traveling jacket.
It had lots of pockets for
bones and balls and little
doggy lollipops.

Mr. Putter and Tabby stood beside Zeke.

They didn't have traveling jackets.

Just a nice blue blanket for naps.

Mr. Putter looked at Mrs. Teaberry.
"You said 'positive,'" he told her.

"Well, the last time I took a train
pets *were* allowed," said Mrs. Teaberry.
"When was that?" asked Mr. Putter.
"1938," said Mrs. Teaberry.

Mr. Putter had to smile.

"Let's just go home," he said.

"We'll have some tea."

"We *can't* go home!"
said Mrs. Teaberry.

"I've brought cards
and games and binoculars
and banana crunchies.
And Zeke's jacket is all filled up!"

"Did you say 'banana crunchies'?"
asked Mr. Putter.
Mrs. Teaberry nodded.
"Like the kind we have on the
Fourth of July?" asked Mr. Putter.
Mrs. Teaberry nodded again.

Suddenly, Mr. Putter couldn't
imagine anything nicer than
being on a train with Tabby
and Mrs. Teaberry and Zeke,
eating banana crunchies.
It would be the best train ride of his life.

"We're not getting any younger,"
Mr. Putter told Mrs. Teaberry.
"I have another idea."

3

Taking the Train

Mr. Putter and Mrs. Teaberry
went home.

One hour later, they went back
to the station and bought their
tickets.

Mr. Putter looked a little
different this time.
This time he had a *very* lumpy
pack on his back.

It was full of little holes,
and sometimes tiny doggy
lollipops fell out.
Mr. Putter just stuck the
lollipops back in and patted
the pack on its head.

Mrs. Teaberry looked a little
different, too.
She was wearing a smock
with very big pockets full of
cards and games and binoculars
and banana crunchies.
And she carried a
picnic basket that purred.
But no one could hear it except
Mrs. Teaberry.

The two old friends got on the
train and found seats by a big window.
The train began to roll.
Chug. Chug. Chug.
Mr. Putter was so happy he thought
he would burst.

And for the next four hours,
he and Mrs. Teaberry had the train
ride of their lives.

Of course, the backpack decided
to crawl under the seat and snore.

And the picnic basket kept batting
at the window shade.

But Mr. Putter and Mrs. Teaberry
just petted them fondly
and fed them banana crunchies
the whole way.

The illustrations in this book were done in pencil, watercolor,
gouache, and Sennelier pastels on 90-pound vellum paper.
The display type was set in Minya Nouvelle, Agenda, and Artcraft.
The text type was set in Berkeley Old Style Book.
Color separations by Bright Arts, Ltd., Singapore
Printed and bound by SCP, China
Production supervision by Stanley Redfern
Series cover design by Kristine Brogno and Michele Wetherbee
Cover design by Brad Barrett
Designed by Arthur Howard and Carolyn Stafford